RED WOLF
COUNTRY

JONATHAN LONDON

illustrated by DANIEL SAN SOUCI

DUTTON CHILDREN'S BOOKS — NEW YORK

Mar. 25. 1996

The publisher has donated a portion of the
proceeds from this book to further the work
of those protecting the red wolf.
—

Text copyright © 1996 by Jonathan London
Illustrations copyright © 1996 by Daniel San Souci
Afterword copyright © 1996 by Roland Smith

Library of Congress Cataloging-in-Publication Data

London, Jonathan, date.
Red wolf country/by Jonathan London;
illustrated by Daniel San Souci.—1st ed.
p. cm.
Summary: Two red wolves hunt, eat, and prepare for the birth
of their pups.
ISBN 0-525-45191-9
1 Red wolf—Juvenile fiction. [1. Red wolf—Fiction.
2. Wolves—Fiction.]   I. San Souci, Daniel, ill.   II. Title.
PZ10.3.L8634Re 1996   [E]—dc20   95-10384
CIP   AC

Published in the United States 1996 by
Dutton Children's Books, a division of Penguin USA Inc.
375 Hudson Street, New York, New York 10014

Designed by Amy Berniker
Printed in Hong Kong   First Edition
10 9 8 7 6 5 4 3 2 1

For my sons, Aaron and Sean,
and for Barbara Kouts, who keeps the dream.
With thanks to Mike Phillips, red wolf specialist. —J.L.

For Joyce Pacheaco, who has spent a lifetime teaching
children to care for all living things.
Special thanks to Roland Smith, who was so generous
with his time and expertise on the red wolf. —D.S.S.

Two red wolves roam
the coastal wetlands.
A rare snow has fallen,
and icicles glitter
in the sweet gum
and loblolly pine.

She-Wolf has a secret
nobody knows.

With her mate, she climbs
a low rise, and as the sun sinks
into clouds of gold and silk,
the coats of the two wolves
flare up like bright red flames.

When twilight falls,
the two mates
stand against the sky
and howl.
It is a haunting song
and for a moment
the world stands still
and listens.

It is the time of the wolves.
They are hungry for deer,
but they'll settle for
a fat gray squirrel
or a dinner of mice.

There below, downwind
in a frozen marsh,
a small dark animal ambles along
in the moonlit southern night.

The red wolves step delicately
through the soft snow.
Gracefully, they drift down
toward the shining pond
and press themselves flat.

They squirm toward
the shadowy creature,
then together bounce up—
and *charge.*

It's a skunk!
The startled wolves skitter
and skate on the slippery ice...

and scramble off into the trees.

Over the following weeks,
as spring begins,
the red wolves hunt
and sometimes eat:
swamp rabbit or fiddler crabs.
Water
    drip
      drip
       drips
and runs in the creeks.
The smell of damp brown earth
fills the air,
and She-Wolf's secret
grows and grows.

She leads as the two mates search
above the cutbanks,
among the trees, under logs,
for a good place to den.

Skirting farms, alert,
sniffing for clues,
they move silently
through their world.

Too close.
A dog barks. The lights
of a farmhouse flick on. The fur
on the nape of their necks
stands up like a lion's mane.

A nervous farmer
raises a rifle. Takes aim.
Focuses She-Wolf
in the crosshairs of his scope

and fires. BAM! A leaf
with a hole in it
spins by her eyes

and both wolves plunge
into a river.

Bullets kick up the water
around their ears. Two alligators
slide down the bank and
slither into the river.

The wolves ride the current,
struggling for air.
Finally, they scrabble up
a muddy bank into thick brush.

Safe at last, they are travelers
in a hurry. They move high
into the hills and farther
from the land
of man.

Days pass.
At last, among the roots
of a huge deadfall tree,
they find the place.

She-Wolf begins to dig and dig,
widening and cleaning
their newfound home.

Soon, the first blooms appear
on the dogwood
and everywhere
the sounds of birds and bees
tremble in the air,
celebrating spring.

And in the den, too, something
is stirring.

Fuzzy and blind
cuddly-warm balls of fur,
nuzzling, hungry for life.

The wolf pups grow
by leaps and bounds—
nibbling berries,
licking mouths, and playing:
flinging around a stiff piece
of rabbit skin to tug on,
while Mother and Father Wolf
take turns watching...

and watching out.

From coastal swamps
to blue-ridge mountains—
for as long as man allows—
theirs is a whole other world—
a world for pups
to grow up in, to mate,
and to have secrets of their own.

Call it: Red Wolf Country.

AFTERWORD

In the 1800s, red wolves could be found throughout the southeastern United States. But by the mid-1960s, the efforts of trappers, hunters, ranchers, and farmers—combined with thoughtless destruction of natural habitat—nearly wiped out the entire population. Only a few wolves remained in Texas and Louisiana. For their own protection, these animals were captured and put into captivity.

By 1980, the red wolf was extinct in the wild. However, within a decade, the captivity-bred wolves would become the nucleus of a remarkable experiment to re-establish the species into its historic range.

In the fall of 1987, several captive red wolves were released at the Alligator River National Wildlife Refuge in eastern North Carolina. It had been over a hundred years since red wolves had run free on North Carolina soil. The wolves did well, and two pairs even produced pups their first year out.

The success at Alligator River led to island re-introduction off the coasts of South Carolina, Mississippi, and Florida. In 1991, a second mainland site was established when red wolves were released in the Great Smoky Mountains National Park in Tennessee.

Currently there are nearly a hundred wolves running free in Red Wolf Country.

ROLAND SMITH
former red-wolf species coordinator
for the U.S. Fish and Wildlife Service